Secrets and Sapphires

For Saskia Ramsey,

with love

ALADDIN

An imprint of Simon & Schuster Children's Publishing Division
1230 Avenue of the Americas, New York, NY 10020
First Aladdin paperback edition September 2016
Originally published in Great Britain by Simon & Schuster UK, Ltd.
Text copyright © 2013 by Michelle Misra and Linda Chapman
Interior illustrations copyright © 2013 by Samantha Chaffey
Cover illustration copyright © 2016 by Christina Forshay
Also available in an Aladdin hardcover edition.
All rights reserved, including the right of reproduction in whole or in part in any form.
ALADDIN is a trademark of Simon & Schuster, Inc., and related logo is a registered trademark of Simon & Schuster, Inc.
For information about special discounts for bulk purchases, please contact
Simon & Schuster Special Sales at 1-866-506-1949 or business@simonandschuster.com.
The Simon & Schuster Speakers Bureau can bring authors to your live event.
For more information or to book an event contact the Simon & Schuster Speakers Bureau at 1-866-248-3049 or visit our website at www.simonspeakers.com.
Designed by Karina Granda
The text of this book was set in Bembo STD.
Manufactured in the United States of America 0816 OFF
2 4 6 8 10 9 7 5 3 1
Library of Congress Control Number 2016941960
ISBN 978-1-4814-5804-7 (hc)
ISBN 978-1-4814-5803-0 (pbk)
ISBN 978-1-4814-5805-4 (eBook)

ANGEL WINGS

Book #3: Secrets and Sapphires

by MICHELLE MISRA

illustrated by SAMANTHA CHAFFEY

ALADDIN

New York London Toronto Sydney New Delhi

Poppy

Ella

Tilly

Archangel
Grace

Jess

Primrose

CONTENTS

CHAPTER 1

New Halos!

"HAVE YOU HEARD THE NEWS?" whispered Ella Brown in excitement, as she sat down next to her friend Poppy in morning assembly.

"What news?" Poppy demanded.

"It's angel-tastic! Someone in our year has . . ."

"Ssh!" Tilly, one of their other friends, hushed them hastily. She nodded to the stage where Archangel Grace, the head of the

Guardian Angel Academy, was waiting for silence. Archangel Grace was a plump angel with wise eyes, enormous gossamer wings, and dark hair that was pulled back into a bun on the back of her head.

Ella fidgeted in frustration on the bench. She was longing to tell Poppy what she had just overheard on the way into the hall but she didn't want to be scolded by Archangel Grace. She pushed her shoulder-length brown hair behind her ears and tried to concentrate.

"Good morning, angels," Archangel Grace said, smiling around at the school. "Now, before I make the morning announcements, I have some good news." She paused. "A third-grade angel has just completed her first halo card!"

"That's what I was going to tell you!"

hissed Ella, elbowing Poppy in the ribs, as excited gasps filled the air.

"Who is it?" whispered Poppy eagerly.

"I don't know!" Ella replied. All the angels at the academy had a halo card and were awarded halo stamps for good behavior. When an angel's halo card was completely filled in, the angel's halo would change color and her wings grow bigger. The white halos all the angels started with changed to sapphire, which changed to ruby and so on, all the way up until the final level was reached—the diamond level. Only the very best, most angelic, angels ever got a diamond halo. Ella longed to have one.

She looked at the rest of the third graders, sitting on the bench. They all had white halos at the moment. Which of them had filled in their card? She knew that it wasn't one of her best friends. Poppy, whose messy blond curls were half hanging out of her ponytail and whose white dress was covered in splotches of ink, was lovely, but she was very clumsy and untidy—neither of which were perfect angel qualities. Tilly and Jess found it easier to get halo stamps—they were both quieter

and more well-behaved—but Ella knew Jess needed another four halo stamps and Tilly another two. Ella touched her own halo card in her pocket and sighed.

One thing was for sure—it definitely wasn't her. She still had ten halo stamps to get!

Halo stamps were awarded for being good and doing kind deeds and, although Ella liked to think she was kind, she definitely wasn't always good! She just couldn't help herself. She always tried her hardest, but somehow she couldn't stop herself from getting into trouble!

"Olivia Starfall, would you like to come up here?" Archangel Grace called over to where a sweet-looking angel with long dark hair and bright-blue eyes was sitting, a little ways from Ella, her ankles crossed and her hands folded neatly in her lap.

Olivia! Of course! Ella wasn't surprised as Olivia stood up, blushing. Olivia was wonderful—always happy to help out if you got stuck, but modest too. She could fly the most perfect loop-the-loop, her silver linings were careful and tidy, and her hair neatly combed. Ella smiled and applauded with the others when Olivia flew up to the stage, her tiny wings fluttering.

As she landed beside Archangel Grace, all of the angels cheered loudly. Well, nearly all of them—Ella caught sight of another angel at the far end of the third-grade bench who didn't look pleased at all. With her golden hair curled into ringlets, big blue eyes and spotless uniform, you would have thought she was a perfect angel, if it wasn't for the scowl on her face. Primrose!

As Primrose leaned in to whisper to the red-haired angel beside her, she covered her mouth with her hand and her eyes narrowed spitefully. Ella sighed. She was sure that Primrose wasn't saying anything nice about Olivia. Ella turned back. Olivia was standing next to Archangel Grace now, her face pink with embarrassment. Archangel Grace raised her wand.

"Good shall be rewarded, virtue too, white halo change to shining blue . . ." She waved her wand in the air three times and a small cloud of glittering silver angel dust cascaded down from it, landing on Olivia's halo. Instantly it turned to deep glowing sapphire, and Olivia's white uniform became the pale blue of a spring sky.

A chorus of gasps and sighs filled the room.

"Wow, isn't that amazing!"

"She looks really beautiful!"

"Oh, I remember getting my sapphire halo when I was a third grader!"

Ella fluttered her own tiny little wings. She wanted to be up on that stage so badly. "I hope I get a sapphire halo soon," she breathed.

As Olivia flew back to her place,

Archangel Grace called for silence again. "And now, on to another matter. A rather less happy one. As you all know, we make our very own angel dust here at the school. It comes from glitter flowers, which are very rare, and it has come to my attention that we're very low on stock. We've planted a new crop of flowers in the school greenhouse but it will take some time before they bloom. Isn't that right, Angel Celestine?" Archangel Grace turned to a pretty, dark-haired teacher who was seated with the other teachers at the back of the stage.

"It is indeed," said Angel Celestine, the gardening teacher. "The crop needs to flower before the glitter can be harvested, which can be tricky. Conditions need to be just right.

Hopefully we should be able to renew our supply of angel dust soon."

Archangel Grace nodded. "And in the meantime, the remaining angel dust must be used sparingly. As you all know, we were going to have the school Spring Picnic next weekend, but I'm going to have to cancel it for the time being to save on magic."

"Oh no . . ." There were groans from around the room.

Ella had never actually been to the Spring Picnic but she'd heard all about it and had been looking forward to it too. Disappointment flooded through her.

Archangel Grace held up her hands again and silence fell. "I know that this will be a huge disappointment to you and I'm really sorry for that, but I am sure you can all understand that we must be sensible. If we run out of angel dust, we won't be able to do any angel magic and that would be a catastrophe."

The angels in the room nodded understandingly.

"We will have the picnic when the flowers can be harvested," said Archangel Grace. "In the meantime, if anyone would like to help out in the greenhouses, looking after the plants, then I am sure Angel Celestine would be very grateful. Now, let us all stand and sing Glad *Tidings and Silver Linings.*"

When assembly was over, Ella filed out of the hall with the other angels. As soon as they were away from the teachers' watchful eyes, she crowded around with her friends.

"Isn't it amazing about Olivia?" burst out Tilly.

"Just glittersome!" said Poppy.

"It'll be us next," joined in Jess, flicking her long dark ponytail over her shoulder.

"Well, maybe you and Tilly." Ella sighed. "But Poppy and I have quite a few more halo stamps to get, don't we, Poppy?"

But Poppy wasn't listening. She was looking at the other side of the room where Primrose was now standing with her arm linked through Olivia's. "Primrose is unbelievable," she said, shaking her head. "Yesterday she made a fuss because she didn't want to sit with Olivia in forgetting spell class because she said Olivia was boring. Now she's acting like they're best friends!"

Primrose simpered as people came up to congratulate the other girl. "Oh, I always knew darling Livvy would be the first to get her sapphire halo," she said loudly. "She's wonderful, isn't she?"

Olivia gave Primrose a very surprised look.

Ella snorted. "If getting a sapphire halo means having Primrose hanging around, then maybe I don't want to fill my halo card after all."

"Ssh! They're coming over!" hissed Jess.

Olivia headed in their direction, with Primrose holding tightly to her arm.

"Congratulations, Olivia." Ella smiled.

"Thanks, Ella," said Olivia shyly. "I can't believe I was the first to get my sapphire halo. It was a real fluke."

"I was just saying how amazing Olivia's sapphire dress and halo look on her, don't you agree?" Primrose gushed. "It's cherub-azing!"

"Er, thank you," said Olivia, clearly flustered by Primrose's attention. "Well, I've got to get something from my dorm. I'll . . . um, see you later." She managed to extract herself from Primrose's grasp and hurried away.

"Don't be long! I'll save you a seat in class!" Primrose called sweetly after her.

"What's going on, Primrose?" Ella demanded. "Since when have you saved Olivia a seat in class?"

Primrose gave her a wide-eyed look. "I'm just being thoughtful."

"Thoughtful!" spluttered Ella. "You've never said two words to Olivia before, but suddenly she gets a sapphire halo and you're her new best friend. I bet you just want to hang around with her now because everyone's giving her lots of attention."

"What a mean thing to say!" Primrose looked shocked. "And when I was only trying to do a kind deed. You know the school handbook says perfect angels are always kind."

She gave Ella a snooty look. "Though why I should expect you to know anything about being the perfect angel, I don't know. How many halo stamps do you still have to get before your card is full, Ella? Is it five? Six? Oh, sorry, I think it's ten, isn't it? Ten!" She rolled her eyes. "And I need . . . hmm, just four. Well, never mind. I'm sure you'll complete your first halo card one day—even if the rest of us have our diamond halos by then! Now, please excuse me or I will be late for class."

Putting her nose in the air, she flew away.

Ella let out a frustrated exclamation. "Halos and wings! Primrose is so annoying!"

"Calm down," said Tilly, putting a hand soothingly on Ella's arm. "She's not worth getting upset over."

"Definitely not," declared Poppy. "You'll fill your halo card up quickly. We all will. Who cares who gets there first?"

"Soon we'll all have sapphire halos like Olivia," said Jess happily. "But Primrose was right about one thing—we'd better not be late for Angel Gabriella or we'll lose some of the halo stamps we've already got!"

"Come on!" Ella cried, whizzing into the air. "Let's go!"

CHAPTER 2

Phoenix Fun!

"Cheep . . ."

Ella pushed back the door to the heavenly animals class to see the smallest, sweetest golden bird sitting on a perch in the middle of the room. Angel Gabriella, their teacher, was standing next to it, gently stroking its feathers.

"Shush . . . quietly," she mouthed the words as Ella and her friends flew in.

"He's a phoenix chick," she explained as they gathered around the table with the other angels. Primrose was already standing there with Olivia. Veronica, Primrose's best friend, was standing to one side looking upset as Primrose whispered to Olivia and giggled with her. Olivia's own best friend, Susie, looked a bit fed up too. Ella saw her edging over to Veronica.

Ella stared at the baby bird. She'd heard about the phoenix—it was a rare, magical bird who laid an egg in a fire when it came to the end of its life and then was reborn from the egg. But she'd never met one. "What's he doing here?" she breathed.

"He's just hatched out of his egg. His name's Jewel," said Angel Gabriella. "I thought you could all draw him. You're used to copying magical animals from books, but what makes an angel a real artist is if she can draw from the real thing."

"Cheep . . ." the baby phoenix called again, as if agreeing with Angel Gabriella, before stretching out his wings and settling down. The little crest on the top of his head wobbled. It looked like a tiny crown.

"He's so cute!" said Jess.

"Can I hold him?" asked Poppy longingly.

"Maybe later," said Angel Gabriella. "But for now could you all stand back a little bit?

I don't want you to crowd him. Can you see how he's starting to change color?"

Ella looked. The phoenix had indeed changed color—the tips of his golden feathers had flushed a ruby red.

"That's because he's feeling frightened," Angel Gabriella explained. "The more frightened he is, the deeper red his feathers will become. We need to put him at ease." She stroked him again, and as the girls stepped farther away, his feathers settled back down to pure gold. "It's really important to look after all creatures, great and small," Angel Gabriella explained. "That's an important part of being an angel."

"I've always been good at looking after animals and birds, Angel Gabriella," Primrose joined in smugly. "At home we found a baby bluebird once. It had dropped out of its nest. I fed him bread and milk every day until he was better."

Ella raised her eyebrows. Primrose had never shown any interest in animals they'd met in heavenly creatures class. It was probably her mother who had looked after the bluebird. If there had even been a bluebird and it wasn't just a made-up story.

"That was very caring of you, Primrose." Angel Gabriella nodded.

"Do I get a halo stamp?" asked Primrose hopefully.

"Not quite yet, Primrose," Angel Gabriella said, laughing. "Though you get marks for trying!"

☆ ☆ 22 ☆ ☆

"I helped a unicorn too once," Primrose went on. "He stayed at my house for weeks and weeks even after he was better. He was just like a great big pet."

"But, Angel Gabriella, aren't you supposed to release animals back into the wild quickly?" Ella asked. She really did know about animals. She had helped a baby fawn out in the woods near her parents' house once and looked after a rabbit with a broken leg. She had pet fish too—sparkly ones that lived in a magical orb in her room.

"That's very true, Ella," said Angel Gabriella. "If an animal is wild, as soon as they're ready to go, we free them. It's better for them that way. We'll talk more about that later, but for now we've got to get on with our life drawing. Everyone, sit at your desks."

The little phoenix settled down again onto the perch in the middle of the table as all of the angels went to their desks.

Ella sat next to Poppy, took out her box of paints from her bag, and placed them carefully by her side before laying out her brushes. But first she had to sketch. As the pencil moved across the paper, she lost herself in her drawing. She looked up for a moment. Poppy was chewing on the end of her pencil. Ella buried herself back in her work. It wasn't until she had nearly drawn the whole phoenix that she stopped and looked up again.

"That's very good, Ella," said Angel Gabriella, coming to a stop beside her. "You've always been really good at copying, but it's a real art to be able to draw from life too. And you've done it so quickly."

"Thank you, Angel Gabriella." Ella smiled, feeling the pride swell up inside her.

"Let's see, Ella," called Poppy. "Turn it around."

Ella did as Poppy had asked.

Poppy grinned. "It's wonderful—but then your drawings always are!"

Angel Gabriella smiled at her. "You can have a halo stamp for being generous with your praise, Poppy. And Ella, you can have one for doing such a good drawing. Take your cards to Archangel Grace's office when you have a moment, girls, and she'll give you your stamps."

Poppy and Ella exchanged delighted looks. Halo stamps were even better when they were totally unexpected! Across the room, Primrose looked fed up. "Angel Gabriella! Come and look at my picture! I've half-finished it!" she called. Angel Gabriella went over.

"So, let's see what you've done," said Ella to Poppy.

"I haven't actually drawn anything yet," admitted Poppy. "I'm not ready. I think I need to take a closer look at Jewel first."

She jumped up, almost tripping over Ella's bag in the process, and went over to the table where the phoenix was. Ella went back to her work. She was so busy that when an alarmed cheep and flapping of wings filled the air, she didn't really notice. But then there was a cry.

"Oh no, what have I done?" Poppy wailed.

Ella looked up quickly. Jewel was on the floor with Poppy crouching beside him.

"What's happened here?" said Angel Gabriella, hurrying over.

"It was Poppy!" cried out Primrose. "I saw her! Poppy dropped Jewel!"

"Did you? Oh, Poppy!" Angel Gabriella swooped down and picked up Jewel. She examined him, carefully laying out each wing and leg while Poppy watched, her face pale. Finally Angel Gabriella put him back on the table with a sigh of relief. "Well, he seems to be unharmed. What were you thinking of, Poppy? Why did you pick him up?"

"I didn't mean to drop him." Poppy hung her head. "I just wanted to have a closer look and he seemed happy, but then he wriggled and flapped his wings . . . and . . . and . . . Oh, why am I so clumsy!"

"Never mind this time," said Angel Gabriella. "Thankfully there's no harm done, but that's why I was saying earlier you have to be so careful with animals. You could have really hurt him. Do you understand?"

"I do, and I'm so very sorry, Angel Gabriella," said Poppy contritely.

"Then we'll say no more about it," said Angel Gabriella. "Now, how far have you gotten with your picture?"

"Not very far." Poppy bit her lip. "In fact, I . . . I haven't even started."

Angel Gabriella sighed. "And class is almost over now. You'll have to stay inside during break to finish it."

"Of course, Angel Gabriella," Poppy said. She walked sadly back to Ella.

"Don't worry. I'll stay and help you, Poppy," Ella whispered.

"That's very kind of you, Ella," said Angel Gabriella who had overheard, although Ella hadn't meant her to. "And for that I'm going to award you a second halo stamp."

"I could stay and help too," Primrose joined in hastily.

"Thank you, Primrose," said Angel Gabriella. "But I think one angel helping Poppy is quite enough."

"I didn't mean I would help Poppy,"

Primrose said. "But my friend hasn't finished her picture yet either. Veronica . . . Veronica," she called across to the desk where Veronica was sitting. "You haven't finished, have you?"

"Yes, I have," said Veronica, looking puzzled.

"No you haven't," said Primrose, going over to her.

At that moment, Jewel let out a little cheep and Angel Gabriella was distracted. Quickly, Primrose pulled an eraser out of her pocket and erased a little bit of Veronica's picture.

"Hey!" cried Veronica.

"Shush," said Primrose, placing a neat little white ballet slipper on Veronica's foot to stop her from saying anything.

"Ouch—that hurts!" Veronica spluttered.

"What was that, Veronica?" Angel Gabriella turned back to the class.

Primrose gave Veronica a sharp look.

"Nothing, Angel Gabriella," Veronica said meekly.

"Okay, now where was I?" Angel Gabriella said. "Oh yes, Veronica . . . Primrose was saying you needed to stay and finish your picture too. Is that right?"

"Yes, Angel Gabriella." Veronica sighed.

"Remember that I said I'd stay and help her," Primrose reminded Angel Gabriella.

"Oh yes, yes," Angel Gabriella said distractedly. "That's very kind."

"So, do I get a halo stamp too?" asked Primrose eagerly.

"Well," Angel Gabriella hesitated. "You're not really supposed to get them for asking, but I suppose on this occasion, it's all right. Primrose, one halo stamp for you as well."

Primrose waited until the teacher had turned away and then flashed Ella a smug look.

"Great!" Ella muttered under her breath to Poppy. "Now we have to put up with Primrose during break time too!"

In no time at all, the classroom was cleared and soon it was just Ella, Poppy, Veronica, and Primrose left in the heavenly animals classroom with Angel Gabriella putting her things away. Ella could see that Poppy was still upset about Jewel and she wanted to cheer her up. She picked up a pencil and balanced it on her upper lip.

"Look!" she whispered, nudging her. Poppy giggled, so Ella did it again, moving her lip and making the pencil move up and down like a mustache.

"Stop it, Ella," said Poppy, trying to ignore her. "I'll never get this finished."

Ella took the pencil and pulled a loose thread off her dress. She tied it onto the end of the pencil like a tail and put the pencil back on her upper lip again.

"Now what are you doing?" Poppy hissed, glancing over.

Ella grinned. "It's a mouse-tache!"

Poppy snorted with laughter. Angel Gabriella looked around. Quickly, Ella stopped what she was doing, but it was too late. The teacher had caught her with the pencil on her lip. Ella groaned inwardly, waiting to be scolded, but Angel Gabriella simply shook her head and smiled.

"I'm not even going to ask you what you're doing, Ella. You know, you might not be the most angelic angel, and you might not have the most halo stamps, but life would certainly be a lot more boring without you around!"

Ella felt taken aback. "What do you mean, Angel Gabriella? Angel Gabriella . . ."

But Angel Gabriella had already left the room. Ella turned to look at Poppy, wondering what her friend had made of the comment, but Poppy was still busy trying to finish her picture. Ella rubbed her forehead. She knew she wasn't a perfect angel, but she wasn't sure she really liked hearing a teacher say it out loud. What exactly had Angel Gabriella meant by it? Had she meant it in a nice way, or had she been scolding her? Maybe she thought Ella would never be a perfect angel?

Primrose flew over. "See, even the teachers know you're a bad angel!" she whispered.

"They know you'll never get a diamond halo. I bet they think you won't even get a sapphire one!"

Ella jumped to her feet and glared at Primrose. But Primrose was already flying swiftly toward the door. "I'm going now!" she called to Veronica.

"What about helping me?" protested Veronica.

Primrose shrugged. "You're almost done. You can finish it on your own. I'm going to get my halo stamp from Archangel Grace."

Ella watched her go. Her mouth felt dry. She knew Primrose was just being mean, but maybe she was right. Maybe her teachers did think she'd never make it to guardian angel level.

"Ella, can you help me draw the wings?" Poppy asked.

"Of course," Ella said, turning her attention to Poppy and the drawing. She tried to forget Primrose's comment, but no matter how hard she pushed it away, it just wouldn't leave her mind. . . .

CHAPTER 3

A Special Guest

A S SOON AS POPPY HAD FINISHED
her drawing, they went outside. Tilly
and Jess had told them that they were going to

spend break time helping in the greenhouses, so they went to find them.

The greenhouses were at the bottom of the garden next to a few small wooden toolsheds. They were very large and ornate, and their panes of glass sparkled in the sun. Ella and Poppy started flying across the grass when they saw Jess and Tilly hurrying over.

"Look! They're carrying something." Ella turned to Poppy. "What is it?"

"I don't know," said Poppy. "But it looks fluffy."

Sure enough, as they got closer, they could see that Jess had an animal in her arms—a brown fluffy bundle with two long ears and a twitchy nose. It had a white chest and pretty white markings on its back in the shape of stars.

"What is it?" Ella called, flying down.

"A celestial bunny," Jess said breathlessly. "We found him over by the greenhouse just when we were about to go in. He's a baby one. He's been hurt."

The little animal's ears moved back and forth and his long whiskers trembled.

"He was really scared when we found him," Tilly said breathlessly. "So I used a calming spell. He's still a bit anxious, but at least he let us pick him up."

"That was a really good idea to use a spell like that," said Ella.

"We used a healing spell too," said Jess. "His paw was bleeding. It's stopped now but the wound is still there."

Ella nodded. Now that she looked, she

noticed that Jess had a few spots of blood on her white dress. "We should get him inside," she said. "Let's find Angel Seraphina. She'll know what to do."

"Good idea," said Poppy. Their class tutor was always full of good ideas.

They hurried back towards the school. As they went in through the back door, they bumped into Primrose coming down the staircase from Archangel Grace's study.

"What have you got there?" she exclaimed and broke off. "Ew!" she squealed dramatically. "Is that blood on your dress, Jess?"

"It's only a few spots," said Jess. "We found an injured bunny. We managed to heal the wound."

"Yuck!" Primrose shuddered.

"Have you see Angel Seraphina?" Poppy asked Primrose.

"No. Why do you want her?"

Ella stared at her. "Maybe for this hurt bunny?"

"Can't you just let it go in the gardens?" said Primrose. "It's only a silly little bunny."

"No we can't just let it go!" Ella said crossly. "It's been hurt."

"I wonder where Angel Seraphina is," said Tilly anxiously.

"Did I hear my name, girls?"

Ella breathed a huge sigh of relief as a beautiful young guardian angel came flying along the corridor, her gossamer wings gleaming, her halo shining with diamonds.

"Angel Seraphina . . . you've got to help.

Tilly and Jess found a bunny . . . a baby one," Ella said breathlessly. "He's been hurt— his paw was bleeding. We've used a calming spell to calm him and a healing one for his

paw," she explained. "Or rather Tilly and Jess did," she said, anxious not to take the credit for something she hadn't done.

"That was quick thinking, angels," said Angel Seraphina. "Let me take a look. . . ."

Jess released her hold on the bunny and, startled, it leaped into Angel Seraphina's arms. Angel Seraphina stroked the little creature and started to check him over.

"You did well to use the healing spell," she said. "The paw's already on the mend. If you hadn't acted so quickly, he would have lost quite a lot of blood."

The baby bunny looked a little less startled now, Angel Seraphina's voice was so calming. Its nostrils had stopped twitching as it started to relax.

"Three halo stamps each, Tilly and Jess," said Angel Seraphina.

"Three halo stamps?" said Tilly, surprised.

"Three WHOLE halo stamps?" Primrose exclaimed. "Just for looking after a bunny!"

"Yes, Primrose . . ." Angel Seraphina looked at the angel in surprise.

"But—" Primrose went to speak but Angel Seraphina held up her hand to silence her and turned back to Jess and Tilly.

"You can collect your halo stamps from Archangel Grace later," she said. "Right now we need to deal with this baby bunny. He'll need to rest for a week before we release him, just to make sure he's healthy and well enough to survive in the wild. He'll need looking after while he's staying with us. Would any of you be kind enough to volunteer?"

"Me ... Me! I'll look after him!" Primrose broke in, even before the final word was out of Angel Seraphina's mouth.

Ella looked surprised. Only five minutes ago Primrose had wanted to let the bunny go in the garden. She also felt a flash of real disappointment. She would have loved to have looked after the sweet little creature.

"Please, please, please, Angel Seraphina," Primrose pleaded. "I'll take really good care of him."

Angel Seraphina smiled. "Thank you, Primrose. And a halo stamp for volunteering."

"Glittersome!" cried Primrose. "Just two more stamps to go!"

"All right, Primrose," said Angel Seraphina, looking slightly displeased. "That's quite enough. What happened to the golden angel rule—*angels must never show off.*"

Primrose looked embarrassed. "I'm sorry, Angel Seraphina," she apologized meekly.

"That's all right, my dear. Now, do we have a name for this bunny?" Angel Seraphina started again.

"Star," burst out Ella who'd been thinking

about it while they'd been talking. She reached out and stroked his fur. "I think he should be called Star—after the markings on his back."

"Very good." Angel Seraphina nodded. "Star it is." She let Ella hold him and give him a cuddle. "Now, I've got a class to get to so, Primrose, why don't you take Star out into the gardens. There's a potting shed over by the greenhouse that should make a nice home for him. It's quiet and cozy and there's plenty of hay nearby. You'll find a spare hutch in there too."

"Of course. I'll take him there right away, Angel Seraphina," Primrose said.

And that was that. As the teacher swept out of the room, Tilly, Poppy, and Jess followed her, leaving Ella and Primrose alone in the room together. Primrose made as if to leave as well.

"Er, aren't you forgetting something, Primrose?" Ella said quickly.

"What?" said Primrose.

"Four legs, two ears, a twitchy nose . . . something you've just promised to take care of, remember." Ella held out the bunny.

"Oh, him." Primrose looked disgruntled.

"Yes, Star! Whatever happened to all the 'please, please, please,'" Ella went on, doing a pretty good impression of Primrose's voice.

"All right, all right." Gingerly, Primrose went to take Star from Ella. She hesitated.

"What's wrong?" said Ella.

"It's just, well, won't his claws scratch my dress?"

"Oh for goodness sake, Primrose." Ella rolled her eyes. "I'll carry him to the shed if you're worried about that."

She cuddled the bunny close and gave him a little scratch behind his ears. His dark eyes gazed trustingly at her. "Come on, Star," she whispered. "Let's get you settled into your new home. . . ."

CHAPTER 4

Sparkling Sapphire

ELLA HURRIED OUT IN THE DIRECTION of the greenhouse with Primrose following. "I don't know why you said you would look after Star if you don't even want to carry him," Ella said. "Did you really only offer so you could get a halo stamp?"

"What's it to you, anyway?" said Primrose haughtily.

Ella cuddled the baby bunny. "I'd have looked after him even if I hadn't gotten any halo stamps for it. Look, why don't you let me care for him, Primrose?"

"No! Then you will get halo stamps!"

Ella only just held on to her temper. She felt like shouting at Primrose, but she'd had halo stamps taken away in the past when she had become angry with the other angel and she wasn't about to risk that again. Not when everyone was so close to getting their sapphire halos.

"Fine," she said abruptly. "Just make sure you look after him well." She kissed the top of Star's head and felt him nestle closer.

They carried on in silence and rounded the corner. The potting shed lay there before them. Ella pushed back the door and stepped inside. It was warm and inviting. Rays of sunlight slanted in through the small window and there was a hutch in one corner, as well as some bags of hay and straw and food. "Can you get the hutch ready while I hold him?" Ella said.

Wrinkling her nose in distaste, Primrose pulled some hay from the bag and started putting it into the main bit of hutch. "No!" Ella stopped her. "The straw goes in there, not the hay. He eats the hay. Haven't you ever looked after an animal like a bunny before?"

"Of course I have!" said Primrose. She shoved the straw and hay in haphazardly. "All done. Put him in."

"Um . . . and what about some water? And food?" Ella said. She saw Primrose's blank look. "Okay, okay, I'll do it." Gently, she put

Star inside the hutch, spreading out the straw into an inviting thick bed with one hand and soothing him with the other. Then she shut the door, filled the water bottle, and put some of the dry food in a little dish.

"This will do for him for now, but he really needs vegetables, too, like carrots and cabbage. Will you make sure you get him some from the gardens?" said Ella.

"Mmm," Primrose said distractedly as she examined her reflection in a little gold hand mirror. "Sure, sure. I'll get whatever he needs."

Ella wasn't convinced. The bunny looked at her and twitched his nose. "You know that he needs feeding three times a day?"

"Yep," Primrose said, inspecting her face and twining a curl around one finger.

"And his water needs changing every day," said Ella.

"Uh huh," said Primrose.

"And he needs lots of cuddling," said Ella.

"Yes, all right, I get it," Primrose said crossly, snapping her mirror shut. "Now, can you leave me alone? I said I'd look after him, didn't I?"

"Okay." Ella hesitated. She was reluctant to leave Primrose, but Angel Seraphina had given Primrose the job so there really wasn't anything she could do. She shouldn't interfere. . . .

Ella flew slowly back in the direction of the Guardian Angel Academy. She couldn't stop thinking about Star. She hated leaving Primrose to look after him. *I'll make sure I keep an eye on her,* she thought. She was so deep in thought that when she reached the door to the Academy, she didn't notice another angel flying out.

"Angels and wings! Watch out, Ella!"

It was Jess!

"Whoops, sorry, Jess," Ella said. "I was miles away." She realized her friend had a massive beam on her face. "You look happy."

☆ ☆ 55 ☆ ☆

"Oh, I am! So happy!" said Jess. "I was just coming to look for you. Come quickly . . . Tilly's got something to show you. She's in the common room. You've got to see it!"

"See what?" Ella said, puzzled.

"I can't believe you haven't realized," said Jess, giggling. "Come on!" She raced back into the school with Ella flying after her. They flew down the maze of hallways before arriving at a door. Ella pushed it back . . . and stopped in her tracks.

"Tilly!" She gasped.

There in front of Ella stood her friend, but instead of her usual pearly white dress, she was head to toe in pale blue and her halo glittered with sapphires!

"Do you like it?" Tilly did a little twirl.

"I've just come back from Archangel Grace's study."

For a moment, Ella couldn't do anything but gape. "Oh . . . w-w-wow!" she stammered. Of course—those extra three halo stamps for helping Star would have filled Tilly's halo card. Ella was overwhelmed with emotions. She was delighted for Tilly, but at the same time, deep down, she felt a stab of jealousy and worry. Tilly had gotten her sapphire halo! Jess would be next. Then Poppy.

What about me? she thought as Angel Gabriella's words came back to her. *What if I never get my sapphire halo?*

Tilly looked at her expectantly. Ella realized she was waiting for her to say something. In fact, so were Jess and Poppy.

"You look, um . . . angel–tastic," she said with a weak smile. Even to her ears she didn't sound very convincing.

Tilly's smile faded slightly. "What's wrong?"

"Nothing," Ella said quickly.

"I thought you'd be really happy for Tilly," Jess said.

"I am!" Ella nodded hard, trying to sound convincing. "Totally and utterly, completely happy. It's really glittery, Tilly." She swallowed, fighting back the jealousy inside. "Good job." She turned hastily away. "I need to get something from the dorm."

"Ella?" Poppy said.

But Ella quickly flew away.

"What's up with Ella?" she heard Jess say.

"Maybe it's this new uniform. Maybe it doesn't look good on me?" she heard Tilly say uncertainly.

Ella blocked her ears and flew on.

"Ella! Wait!" Poppy came after her. Ella pretended not to hear. She was better at flying than Poppy and she zoomed on ahead.

"Ella!"

Poppy was panting by the time she caught up with Ella at the dorm door, and her blond curls were even messier than usual. "Okay, what's going on? I know you heard me back there. Why didn't you wait? And why were you so strange with Tilly?"

Ella opened the door and hurried inside the dorm. It looked just as pretty as ever with their rainbow-colored cloud beds floating in the air and a golden dove cooing from above the door. A large oval window looked out on to the grounds. Ella went over to the window and gazed out of it.

"Ella?"

"Don't you care that Tilly has her sapphire halo and we don't?" Ella burst out, swinging around.

Poppy looked at her in astonishment. "Why should I care about that? Tilly's a much better angel than I am. I always knew she would get her sapphire halo before me."

Ella sighed. She knew that what Poppy was saying made sense—it just made her feel all the more terrible for feeling jealous and not being nicer to Tilly back in the common room.

"It's not a competition, Ella," Poppy said softly. "We'll all get a sapphire halo in the end if we try hard enough."

Ella nodded slowly. "You're so much nicer than me," she said miserably. "I'm an awful angel!"

"No you're not," said Poppy, giving her a

big hug. "You're honest, that's all. And that's an important angel quality too, remember? Angel Seraphina's always saying that."

Poppy's words were a huge comfort, but Ella still felt bad. Poppy wasn't jealous, so why should she be? She really was a terrible friend and a terrible angel. *It'll be Jess who gets a sapphire halo next*, an anxious little voice in her head said. Then Poppy. *I'll be the only one with a white one.*

"Come on, let's go back and find the others," said Poppy.

Ella took a deep breath and followed her slowly out the door.

CHAPTER 5

A Discovery

ELLA TRIED VERY HARD TO BE HAPPY for Tilly over the next few days, but the jealous feelings wouldn't go away. She felt really bad about it. A good angel wouldn't ever have such horrible feelings, she was sure. It made her much quieter than usual. Luckily her friends were busy and didn't notice too much. They were all helping out in the greenhouses with the glitter plants whenever they could—watering them, giving them flower food, making sure they

were turned regularly so that their leaves all got an equal amount of sun. Everyone in the school wanted the plants to flower so that the glitter dust supplies could be renewed—and so that the Spring Picnic could happen!

Unfortunately, Angel Celestine couldn't tell them exactly when that would be. Apparently, all you could do was care for the plants and wait for conditions to be exactly right and then the flowering would begin.

Jess, Tilly, and Poppy loved helping in the greenhouses, and went every break and at lunchtime, but Ella wasn't so excited. She thought plants were boring. Whenever they went to the greenhouses she would look at the little potting shed where Star was being kept and wish she could be looking after him instead. But whenever she tried to go in and see him, she found that the door was locked. Strangely, she never seemed to see Primrose there, but a few days after Star had been found, she did overhear Primrose at lunchtime telling Angel Seraphina that she was visiting the bunny four times a day and he was doing well. Angel Seraphina gave her another halo stamp for all her care and attention. Ella felt her heart twist. Now Primrose just needed one more to get her sapphire halo—just like Jess!

Remember what Poppy said, it's not a competition, Ella reminded herself firmly, as she walked away from Primrose and Angel Seraphina.

She found Poppy, Jess, and Tilly sitting in the sun, eating their lunches.

"What have you got there, Jess?" Ella asked, sitting down by Jess and seeing a large scrapbook beside her.

"Oh, it's nothing—just a project I've started," said Jess. "On glitter flowers."

"Have I missed something?" said Poppy in alarm. "Are we all supposed to be doing that? Is it homework?"

"No, don't worry." Jess grinned. "It was just something I wanted to do."

"Phew!" said Poppy.

"What sort of project?" Ella asked curiously.

"Well . . ." Jess hesitated, looking a little embarrassed. "I had this idea that if I put together all the things we know about glitter flowers, it might help us for next time—to stop us from running out again. Everyone seems to be very vague about when they flower and why. Angel Celestine just says that with enough care and love they'll eventually bloom—but she also says that in special conditions they can flower sooner. I thought if I wrote everything down it might help."

"It's a glittersome idea," said Tilly.

"Yeah," said Ella. She swallowed. It was a really good idea, and if Jess did it well it would be just the sort of thing to get her the last halo stamp she needed!

She instantly felt angry with herself. That wouldn't be why Jess was trying to do it. She wasn't like Primrose. She was just genuinely trying to be helpful. *But even so,* the little voice said, *she might get her sapphire halo and you've still got eight stamps left to go!*

Feeling uncomfortable, Ella got to her feet. "I'm going to go for a little walk," she said.

"Do you want some company?" Poppy asked.

Ella shook her head. She saw her friends glance at one another in concern. She knew they were starting to worry about why she was so subdued. "I'll catch you later!"

She headed off before they could come with her. She walked down towards the greenhouses and stopped by Star's shed. As usual it was locked. Ella sighed as she rattled the door. She would have loved to have cuddled the baby bunny. She sniffed suddenly. A strange, not very pleasant smell was coming from the slightly open window. What was it?

She fluttered her wings and flew up to the window. It was open just a crack. As she peered in, she let out a loud gasp. The hutch was filthy! Not only that, but the water bottle was nearly empty and she could see the food bowl was bare too. Pitifully, the baby bunny scratched at the dirty straw in his cage. So much for Primrose checking on him four times a day!

Ella had to do something. She managed to get her hand in through the open window and undo the clasp, then she pushed the window open fully and climbed inside. Her white dress snagged on the wood and as she pulled her way through, she got covered in dust, but she didn't care. She flew down to the floor and rushed to the hutch. "Oh, you poor thing," she said, looking at the sad little bunny. She opened the door and let him out, fetching him a bowl of food. While he hungrily started to eat, she cleaned all the dirty straw out, shoving it into an old bag and replacing it with fresh straw. Then she added hay to his living compartment and refilled his water bottle. The horrible musty smell in the air was going away now that the window was open fully.

"Oh, Star. Primrose hasn't been looking after you at all, has she?" she said, crouching down on the floor and getting even more dusty.

The little bunny looked at her anxiously. She gently picked him up and cuddled him to her. She could feel his tiny heart pitter-pattering, his fur was velvet soft against her cheek.

She stroked him over and over again until she felt him relax and then she put him back in his hutch with a bowl of food. "Don't worry," she whispered to him. "I won't let Primrose get away with this!"

She felt furious. How could Primrose have forgotten to feed him? Why hadn't she been looking after him?

"I'll be back later to check on you, Star," she promised. "And I'll bring you some carrots. But first there's someone I need to talk to."

Ella flew back up to the window and wriggled out. It didn't take her long to find

Primrose. She was with Veronica, Olivia, and Susie on the other side of the grounds, playing angel volleyball. She caught sight of Ella and raised her eyebrows.

"Are you entering a dress-as-a-scarecrow competition? Or is it look-like-you've-been-dragged-through-a-bush-backward day?" She smirked.

Ella paid no attention. "How *could* you, Primrose?"

"How could I what?" Primrose said, but a guilty flush tinged her cheeks.

"I want a word with you," said Ella. "Away from here. Or I can say what I've got to say in front of everyone if you like?" she added.

"Er, no, all right, I'm coming," Primrose said hastily.

They stopped a little way off from the
others.

"I went to see Star just now," Ella said.

"So?" Primrose looked defensive.

"His hutch was dirty, he didn't have any

food, and there was only a trickle of water in his water bottle!" Ella exclaimed furiously.

"All right, all right," said Primrose. "Keep your halo on!" She glanced at the others who were looking at them curiously.

"You promised to look after him," Ella hissed. "You even got an extra halo stamp for it! I heard you telling Angel Seraphina all about how often you were visiting him. But you haven't been looking after him at all!"

Primrose looked sulky. "I've been to see him once."

"Once isn't enough—and you haven't cleaned his cage out at all!"

"So, what are you going to do about it?" A wary look crossed Primrose's face. "I suppose you're going to tell."

Ella hesitated. "No," she said, through gritted teeth. "I'm not." As much as she would have liked to, she didn't like people who tattled. "But I want the key to the shed. You're not to keep it locked anymore."

Primrose pulled out a small metal key from her pocket and handed it to her.

"And you'd better start looking after him properly," said Ella. "This is your last chance. If you don't care for him, I WILL do something about it."

"Oh, halos and wings, I'm so scared!" said Primrose, getting some of her usual confidence back now that she knew Ella wasn't going to tell. She flounced off towards the others who had started playing again without her. Ella stared after her. What was she going to do? She didn't want to tell Angel Seraphina but what if Primrose didn't look after Star any better?

No problem, she thought, her fingers closing on the key. *I'll just look after him myself!*

CHAPTER 6

Angel Secrets

ELLA HEADED BACK TO STAR'S SHED. As she got close to it, she saw Jess walking towards the greenhouses. "Jess!" she called, keen to make up for being quiet earlier.

Jess smiled and waited for her. "Hi!" She blinked as she saw the state of Ella's clothes.

"Goodness, what have you been doing?"

"Climbing through a window into Star's shed!" Ella quickly told Jess what had happened.

Jess was horrified. "But that's terrible!"

Ella nodded. "I know, but at least I found out, and I've got the key now so if Primrose doesn't look after him, I will."

"Shouldn't we tell Angel Seraphina that Primrose hasn't been taking care of him?" asked Jess.

"That would be tattling," Ella pointed out.

They looked at each other. Jess hesitated and then nodded. "I suppose."

"The important thing is that Star gets looked after properly from now on," said Ella. "Anyway, what are you doing here?" she said, seeing the sketchbook in her friend's hand. "Are you doing more of your project?"

"Yes. I thought I could draw one of the flowers," Jess said. "I tried drawing one from memory, but it was useless, and then I remembered what Angel Gabriella said in heavenly animals—about how sometimes it's easier to sketch from life, so I thought I'd come here and give it a try."

"Let's see the drawing you've done so far," Ella said.

Jess turned the pad around.

"It's . . . um . . . it's . . ."

"Terrible." Jess sighed. "I know. I'm bad at drawing!"

Ella chewed her bottom

lip. The flower looked more like an oak tree! She felt the offer to help rise to her lips. She had helped Jess before with her drawings. *But that was before Jess only needed one more halo stamp to get her sapphire halo*, the little voice in her head said. Ella hesitated. She wanted to help, she really did. But . . . but . . .

"I'll go and have another try," said Jess cheerfully. "Maybe Angel Gabriella's right and I'll do a better drawing with the plant in front of me. See you later, Ella!"

She went on. Ella watched her. Her mouth opened and then shut again as she almost called her friend's name and then stopped herself. Jess went into the greenhouse.

Ella sucked in her breath. She should have offered to help. She knew she should.

It was jealousy again and she disliked herself for it. She was so lost in her thoughts that she didn't notice Angel Seraphina coming toward her.

"Penny for your thoughts." Angel Seraphina smiled.

"Oh, hello, Angel Seraphina," said Ella, jumping guiltily.

"Is everything okay, Ella?"

"Yes, everything's fine."

"It's just that you've seemed quieter than your usual self this week," said Angel Seraphina, her eyes meeting Ella's.

"Have I?" said Ella, startled that someone had noticed. "Oh. Well, I'm all right." She could hardly admit to a guardian angel—and a teacher at that—what she was feeling.

"Is it because Tilly has her sapphire halo?" Angel Seraphina said gently.

Ella stared. Could Angel Seraphina read her mind? "Oh, Angel Seraphina," she burst out, unable to hold it all in anymore. "I don't know why, but I can't stop feeling jealous. I can't bear it. I'm a useless angel. And a terrible friend too!"

Angel Seraphina smiled. "Ella Brown, you are neither of those things."

"I am," said Ella miserably.

"No you're not." Angel Seraphina looked thoughtful. "You know, Ella, I knew an angel once who felt exactly the same way as you. Every time one of her friends went up a level before her, it ate her up inside. She didn't tell anyone, of course, but she hated herself for it."

"Really?" said Ella, surprised to hear that

another angel could possibly have felt the same way as her.

"Really," said Angel Seraphina. "And when her own best friend got a ruby halo before her—well that was the very worst."

"And did that angel make it to the ruby stage herself?" asked Ella.

"She did indeed," said Angel Seraphina. She brushed down her dress and smiled. "She even made it to Guardian Angel level."

"You mean YOU?" said Ella, suddenly understanding what Angel Seraphina was trying to tell her.

"Yes, me." Angel Seraphina laughed. "Remember, I was a trainee guardian angel once too and when I was at school I learned the important lesson that it's not how you *feel* inside that matters but how you *act* on those feelings."

Ella frowned. It definitely put a different take on things.

"I hope knowing that helps you, Ella," said Angel Seraphina. "Now, I want to go and see how the glitter flowers are coming along. Do you want to come with me?"

Ella nodded. As she followed the teacher into the greenhouse, she realized that what Angel Seraphina had just said made perfect sense. You couldn't help the feelings you had— feelings just happened in your head. It was how you acted that made you good or bad.

They found Jess inside, sketching. "How's it going?" Ella asked, going over to her as Angel Seraphina walked around, inspecting the flowers with their tightly closed buds.

"Look!" Jess sighed and held up her pad. "Maybe if you can draw like Angel Gabriella then it's easier to draw from life, but not if you're as useless as me."

"Don't be silly, you're not that bad," said Ella. "First of all you need to look at the proportions of the plant. At the moment the leaves you've drawn are much too small and the stem too thick. Why don't you start again and I'll help you?"

They sat side by side, not even noticing when Angel Seraphina left the greenhouse, both engrossed in the picture. With Ella's help, Jess began to draw a plant that looked much more realistic. When the drawing was finally finished, she beamed.

"Oh, it looks perfect now, Ella," said Jess. "Thank you so much. When I hand my project in, I'll tell Angel Celestine how much you helped me."

"Don't be silly, Jess," Ella said. "This is your project. You did the drawing, I just gave you some advice."

"But you might get a halo stamp. . . ."

"I didn't do it because I wanted a halo stamp," Ella said. "I just did it for you."

Their eyes met. For a moment Ella thought the light in the greenhouse seemed to glow even more brightly. She blinked and everything was back to normal.

"Thank you for helping me," Jess said, standing up.

"I'm just glad I could," Ella said. They smiled at each other and, linking arms, they left the greenhouse together.

CHAPTER 7

Uncovered!

FOR THE REST OF THE DAY, ELLA WENT back and forth from the school to the shed to look after Star. There was neither sight nor sound of Primrose, but Ella didn't care about that. She was really enjoying looking after the little bunny herself. She felt so much happier since her talk with Angel Seraphina. Jess's project was almost finished and Ella was sure she would get a halo stamp for it when she handed it in, but suddenly she realized she felt okay about that. Of course she still wanted a sapphire halo herself, but Angel Seraphina had made her feel much better. She might not be one of the *first* to get a sapphire halo but if she really tried to be good, she would fill her card and still get one. Just like Angel Seraphina had when she'd been younger.

Ella was much more her usual self with her friends that evening, and when Jess handed her project in to Angel Seraphina and got her final halo stamp, Ella celebrated with them all.

She slept really well that night and in the morning she bounced out of bed, eager to go and see Star before classes started.

"Where are you off to?" Poppy asked as Ella pulled on her dress.

"To see Star."

"I'd like to see him too," said Poppy, who was still in bed. "I'll follow you down there when I'm dressed."

"Me too!" said both Tilly and Jess.

Ella smiled and set off. "See you all there!"

She flew towards the potting shed, humming to herself. As she opened the door, Star sat up and twitched his ears. He looked really happy to see her. "Hello, Star!" Ella opened the door

to the hutch and he hopped out onto her lap. She cuddled him and then set to work cleaning him out. She had just finished and sat down to give the bunny another cuddle when there was a noise behind her that made her start.

"Oh, Angel Seraphina, it's only you," Ella said, smiling.

"Ella! I hadn't expected to find you here." Angel Seraphina looked surprised. "I saw the door open and thought Primrose must be in here. Is she around?"

"Er, I'm not sure. I haven't seen her," said Ella truthfully.

"Well, I'm sure she'll be here soon," said Angel Seraphina. "It looks like she's been looking after Star very well." She gave an approving look at the clean hutch.

"Here I am!" a breathless voice came from behind. It was Primrose. "Just doing my daily duty," she said, beaming. "Hello, Star, my sweetheart."

The little bunny shrank back, nuzzling farther into Ella's arms, his dark eyes wary.

Primrose ignored his alarm. "Star, it's me, come to Mommy," she crooned, reaching out. The bunny scrambled away, pushing against Ella's chest.

"Just wait a minute, let him settle down," Ella said, aware that Angel Seraphina was watching, a slightly puzzled frown on her face. Ella gave Primrose a pointed look, wanting to say, "let him get used to you first," but she didn't want to make it obvious that the bunny wasn't used to Primrose at all.

Impatiently, Primrose tried to pull him away from Ella. Star panicked and scrambled in her arms.

"Ow!" Primrose squealed, dropping him. "He scratched me!"

Star raced for the door and dashed out of the shed.

"Quick!" said Ella.

The angels hurried out of the shed and saw Star running in and out of the borders of the vegetable patch.

"Oh, dear we've got to catch him," said Angel Seraphina. "As he knows you best, you should go after him, Primrose."

"Me? Right . . . um . . ." Primrose swallowed as she went after the bunny. "Here, bunny. Nice bunny!" she cooed.

But every time Primrose got anywhere near him, Star ran away again. He started to look more and more anxious, darting this way and that with Primrose pursuing him. Ella couldn't bear it any longer. She pulled a carrot out of her pocket and headed over. She crouched down in a sitting position.

"Here, Star," she soothed. "Come to me."

The baby bunny's little nose sniffled at Ella's offering. Would it work? Would he go to her? Ella held her breath as the baby bunny took one tentative step in her direction.

"That's it," Ella crooned. "Easy does it."

One step . . . two . . . and Star was easily within Ella's reach.

"It's just a fluke!" Primrose said hastily. "I could have gotten him. I could have . . ."

"Be quiet, Primrose!" Angel Seraphina spoke sharply.

"There's a good boy." Ella smiled as Star drew closer and closer before he finally jumped into her arms for the waiting carrot. Ella stroked him and he nestled into her.

"Well done, Ella." Angel Seraphina smiled. Primrose looked like she was going to explode!

Once Star was settled back into his hutch with the door locked, Angel Seraphina turned to the two angels. "Is someone going to tell me exactly what is going on here? I want to know the truth."

Ella didn't say anything. Primrose remained silent too.

"Well, it's clear to me that Ella has been

helping you with Star," said Angel Seraphina. "Is that what's been going on?"

"Well, just a *little* bit," said Primrose.

"JUST A LITTLE BIT!" Angry voices came from behind. Ella looked around. Her friends—Poppy, Tilly, and Jess—were in the doorway and they looked furious. "Tell her, Ella."

"Well, I . . ." Ella didn't know what to say.

"Primrose didn't look after him properly at all," Poppy burst out. "Luckily, Ella realized that and she cleaned his hutch and looked after him all day yesterday. She was going to look after him for the rest of the week without saying anything."

Tilly nodded. "She's the one who really cares about Star! That's why he likes her."

Angel Seraphina's eyes narrowed, and

for an angel, she looked pretty furious. "Is this true, Primrose? Is this what has been going on?"

"Well, um . . . maybe," Primrose mumbled, not able to meet Angel Seraphina's eyes.

The older angel looked angry. "That's it! I'm not impressed by this behavior. Not at all. Not only did you promise to look after Star, but you deceived me into thinking you were doing a good job of it too. You have neglected one of our heavenly animals and taken halo stamps for your efforts! I'm going to have to take all those stamps away, and another two for dishonesty."

Primrose looked aghast. "But, Angel—"

"No buts," said Angel Seraphina. "Ella, Primrose's stamps will go to you."

"To me?" said Ella, surprised.

"Yes, to you—not only for looking after Star, but for showing real angel qualities by not tattling and looking after him just to make him happy. There's a lot of good in you, you know, Ella Brown," she said. "An awful lot of good. Make sure you remember that."

Her friends gave a loud cheer and Ella looked embarrassed, but there wasn't time for that as, just at that moment, there was a loud shout from outside—right by the greenhouse. It was Angel Celestine!

"Over here!" she cried, running out the greenhouse door. "Come and see!"

The angels rushed over to the greenhouse and stepped inside. They couldn't see what

Angel Celestine was talking about at first. But then they couldn't believe their eyes. Not one, not two, not three, but ALL of the glitter flowers had burst into full sparkling bloom!

CHAPTER 8

Spring Picnic!

I JUST CAN'T UNDERSTAND IT," SAID Angel Celestine. "The only thing that would make the flowers bloom like this—other than patience and a whole lot of love and care—is if someone does a perfectly unselfish deed near the plants, but no one's been in to see them today."

"That is strange," said Angel Seraphina. "I wonder how it could have happened."

Jess gasped. "This deed? It has to be completely unselfish?"

"Completely and utterly," said Angel Celestine. "The person can't be hoping to gain from it in any way."

"Then I know who's responsible," Jess cried. "Ella, don't you see—it was YOU!"

"Me," said Ella, frowning. "But how?"

"Yesterday afternoon," went on Jess, her eyes shining. "We were in here—and you did the most unselfish thing possible—you helped me with my glitter flower project, remember? And you did it knowing that it would get me the final stamp for my halo card and get me a sapphire halo—the very thing that you wanted yourself."

"I did?" said Ella, feeling embarrassed.

"Yes, you did," said Jess. She turned to Angel Seraphina. "I didn't tell anyone that

Ella had helped me with my project, but she did—she made all my illustrations work. I should have said. I didn't really earn that last halo stamp myself," she said.

"Oh, but you did," said Angel Seraphina. "The drawings were lovely, but I really awarded it to you for all the information you had gathered."

"Really?" Jess said shyly.

"Yes," said Archangel Grace. "And now that the flowers have bloomed there's no longer a glitter shortage, so the Spring Picnic can go ahead this weekend after all!"

"Hooray!" All of the angels let out a loud cheer, each giving Ella a thump on the back.

Ella turned to them and grinned. "I might

not have all my halo stamps this time, but I don't care! I know I'll get them in the end!"

The Spring Picnic was a huge success. Rugs were laid out covering the grass in Archangel Grace's private garden, and all sorts of delicious

angel foods were piled high—cloudberry cookies, honey sandwiches, towers of rainbow jelly, and big jugs of star fruit lemonade. There were even lollipops hanging on the trees. All of the angels were happy. Well, apart from Primrose. She was sitting on her own, sulking.

Veronica had become really good friends with Susie and Olivia and now they were playing tag together.

"Whoo-hoo," cried Poppy, as she slid down a massive rainbow slide in the middle of the garden. "Isn't this great!"

"The best!" Ella cried, as she swooped around with enormous pink and lilac butterflies that fluttered through the air.

"Oh look, Ella, over there," cried Jess.

Ella looked over to the other side of the grass to where Jess was pointing, and there she saw a little familiar furry face with long ears and whiskers twitching. Star! They had released the baby bunny back onto the grounds the day before, but he kept coming back to check on them!

"I think he might be around for quite some time." Tilly grinned.

"Just like my friends!" said Ella, grinning as she linked arms with Poppy, who linked arms with Tilly, who linked arms with Jess. "Together, forever!"

Read on for a sneak peek
at Ella's angel-tastic
adventures in:

MICHELLE MISRA

ANGEL
WINGS

Rainbows and Halos

CHAPTER 1

Brilliant Baking!!

GLITTERSOME!" ELLA BROWN LOOKED over Poppy's shoulder at the perfect heart-shaped cookies she was icing.

"Thanks, Ella!" Poppy pushed back her messy blonde curls. "For once I've done something more neatly than you!" she teased.

As Ella looked down at her own cookies, she could see exactly what her friend meant. The icing was all wobbly, the shape looked more like a square than a heart, and the cookies were all splotchy! Still, it was only their first angel baking lesson.

"I guess they don't need to look good to taste good," Ella said hopefully.

"Well, we'll soon find out!" Poppy closed her eyes and took a bite of one her cookies. "I wish for happy thoughts . . . ooh, that's lovely," she smiled. "Butterflies and bluebirds!"

Ella took a bite of one of hers. "Ooh, yum," she squealed as she munched. "Delicious. It tastes like strawberries and cream!"

"Don't forget to make a wish before you

finish it!" Poppy reminded her quickly.

Ella closed her eyes and thought her wish.

"What did you wish for?" asked Poppy curiously.

"That it wasn't so hot!" sighed Ella. "It's baking in here."

Poppy nodded, fanning herself. "I'm melting like ice cream!"

"I've never known it be so sunny," said Ella. It had been like this all summer so far. They were in the middle of a heatwave at the Guardian Angel Academy.

"I hope the weather changes soon," Poppy said. "Or we'll be boiled alive at sports day next week! Imagine trying to run and jump and fly in this heat?"

Ella nodded and was just about to take

another bite of her cookie when their teacher came rushing over.

"Ella! What are you doing?" she cried out. "Halos and wings! There'll be nothing left. We're supposed to be icing the cookies, not eating them!"

"Whoops, sorry Angel Seraphina," Ella grinned. "They are delicious, though."

"Oh, maybe I'll just try a little bit!" said Angel Seraphina. She took one of the cookies. "Mmm, delicious indeed. Zero marks for neatness, Ella, but ten out of ten for taste!"

Ella glowed. She really liked her teacher.

Angel Seraphina turned to the rest of the class. "Let's get cleaned up!" she called out. "The sooner we clear away, the sooner we can go outside and get some fresh air. Now, Poppy, can you bring your cookies into the other room. I want to have a proper look at them."

Ella gazed out of the window to where a group of fourth graders were playing angel volleyball. Multi-colored butterflies swooped over the lawns and the gentle hum of bees filled the air.

She turned and almost knocked over an angel hurrying past. "Sorry, Tilly!" she gasped.

"No problem." Tilly had light brown hair and was wearing a sapphire uniform. "I'm just trying to catch ONE . . . OF . . . THESE . . . 'The words came out in short bursts as she reached up to try and catch a chocolate cupcake that was whizzing above her head.

Ella fluttered her wings and rose up in the air, grabbing the cake. "Gotcha!" She grinned. "Here you go." She handed it over to Tilly.

"Thanks, Ella!"

Jess, an angel with a long dark ponytail, joined them. "Have you got them all?" she asked.

"Yes, Ella just caught the last one."

"Thanks, Ella," Jess smiled. Tilly and Jess were the other two angels that made up a dorm with Ella and Poppy. The four of them were the best of friends.

Ella looked at the flying cupcake in Tilly's hands. Its wings were beating frantically. "Flying cupcakes are hard to make. You've done really well. My wish cookies are a mess. They looked up to where the sun was still beating down. Tilly held the cupcake up to examine it. "It was really all Jess's cooking not mine. But it does look good."

"Let me see," said Ella. She took it and her eyes glinted mischieviously. Angel Seraphina had gone to the other cooking room with Poppy. "Hey, it really flies well!" she said as she let it go. "Look!"

It hovered above her head before shooting off and whizzing around the room.

"Ella!" Tilly and Jess exclaimed.

"Oh, no. We'll never catch it now!" said Tilly.

Ella giggled as Tilly flew into the air and chased after it. Every time she neared the cupcake, it jetted off in another direction, as if it was playing a game of tag with her! Tilly

finally managed to grab it. "I'll get you for that, Ella Brown," she called as she swooped down. "Food fight!"

And, picking up the nearest spoon, she splattered Ella with some gloopy cake mixture.

"Okay!" cried Ella, grinning, splattering Tilly in return.

"Stop it! You'll ruin my dress!" a voice behind them screeched.

Ella spun round. Primrose! She might have guessed! The most perfect-looking angel in the school was also the most odious. She looked Ella up and down with a snooty look. "Haven't you forgotten the school rules? "Angels should strive to be neat and tidy at all times.'"

Ella raised her eyebrows at Tilly and then splattered her friend again. Tilly ducked and it hit Jess head on.

"Ella!" Jess shrieked and then she burst out laughing.

"Well, I suppose that at least it wasn't my dress that was spoiled," sniffed Primrose. "Not that I'll be in this babyish white dress for much longer," she said, doing a smug little twirl.

"Yes, we know," Ella sighed crossly. "You've only got one more halo stamp to get before you go up to sapphire level."

All of the angels started at the Academy with plain white dresses and halos. As they did angelic things, they were awarded halo stamps and went up levels. White to sapphire, sapphire to ruby, and so on, until they reached gold and then gold became diamond. That made you a Guardian Angel. Not only that but your wings grew at every stage until finally they were the largest, downiest of wings that changed with every color of the rainbow.

"So how many halo stamps have you got left to get you to sapphire level, Ella?" Primrose asked, her eyebrows arched.

"You already know the answer to that," said Ella with a scowl.

It was a bit of a sore subject. While most of the first years had already got their sapphire halos, Ella still had to earn hers. Tilly and Jess had gone up a level last term and Poppy, like Primrose, was only one halo stamp away. Ella still had another three stamps to go. It seemed like a never-ending task!